*Disney*

# 5-MINUTE MINNIE TALES

*Disney* PRESS

Los Angeles • New York

# CONTENTS

# MINNIE'S SCAVENGER HUNT

One beautiful spring morning, Minnie woke up to find a surprise waiting for her. Someone had slipped an envelope under her front door!

"What could this be, Figaro?" Minnie asked. She opened the envelope and pulled out a note.

"Why, it's a secret scavenger hunt!" Minnie cried. "And look! The first item on the list is a picnic basket."

Minnie opened the closet and pulled out a soft blanket. She also took out a large basket.

"I can use this to carry everything," she said.

Placing the blanket in the basket, Minnie waved good-bye to Figaro and headed outside.

Minnie checked the list again. "Item number two: three cucumbers," she read.

Minnie knew just what to do. She went to her garden and chose several of the big, green vegetables. Adding them to her basket, she went to find the next item on her list.

"Hmmm . . ." said Minnie. "A stick as tall as I am. There's only one place to go for that!"

Minnie turned and was headed for the woods when she ran into Goofy.

"Hiya, Minnie," Goofy said. "What are you doing?"

Minnie was about to show Goofy her basket when she remembered that the scavenger hunt was a secret. Then she noticed that Goofy was hiding some blueberries behind his back. Maybe he was part of the scavenger hunt, too!

"I'm just out for a walk," Minnie replied finally. "I'll see you later, Goofy!" And with that, she hurried off into the woods.

Soon Minnie had found the third item on her list.
In the distance, she heard rushing water.

"I wonder what that is," Minnie said, and she went
to find out.

A few minutes later, she came upon a stream. Nearby was a
patch of green plants with red peeking out from underneath.
Minnie bent down to examine them.

"Strawberries!" she exclaimed. "These are the next item on
my list!"

Minnie picked the strawberries and added them to her basket. The she checked her list again. The next item was five smooth stones. "Then stream is a great place to find smooth stones!" Minnie said.

Minnie left her basket on the shore and waded into the water. In no time she had found five smooth rocks on the streambed.

Minnie only had one item left on her list: a yellow flower. But as she looked around, she realized she was lost. She had wandered too far into the woods!

Minnie walked in one direction for a while, but somehow she just ended up back at the brook.

"Oh, no!" she said. "I'll never finish the scavenger hunt if I can't get out of the woods!"

Suddenly, Minnie spotted something on the ground.

"Blueberries! Goofy was picking these. Some must have fallen out of his bag," Minnie realized. "If I follow them, they should lead me back to the path and out of the woods!"

Minnie followed the trail over a log, through a bush, and under a heavy branch, until finally she found the path—and a patch of daffodils!

"A yellow flower!" Minnie cried. "That's the last item on my list!"

Minnie picked one of the flowers and added it to her basket. Then she happily skipped down the path. As she arrived at the park, Minnie saw her friends appear with their own baskets.

"Surprise!" Mickey said. "I left each of you a list of items to collect. Now we can combine them and have a party!"

Minnie smiled as she and her friends got to work. She laid down her picnic blanket. Donald tied balloons to a nearby tree. Daisy got out a vase, and the friends all added the flowers they had picked. Finally, Mickey cut up the berries and vegetables for a delicious lunch.

The five friends played in the park for the rest of the afternoon. Donald used Minnie's stick to hit the piñata Mickey had brought. Minnie and Daisy played hopscotch with Minnie's stones and Daisy's chalk. And Goofy made a funny hat from Donald's newspaper. It was a wonderful party and the perfect spring day!

# MINNIE'S SUMMER DAY

**M**ickey Mouse was relaxing in his living room when, suddenly, the doorbell rang. Mickey opened the door to find a very upset-looking Donald.

"What's wrong, Donald?" Mickey asked.

Donald sighed. "It's too hot at my house. Can I stay with you for the day?"

Mickey happily invited Donald inside. And
then Minnie . . . and Goofy . . . and Daisy! The friends
were just deciding what to do with their day when—*pop!*
Mickey's air-conditioning broke!

"Maybe there will be a breeze outside," said Minnie.
But there was no breeze. Just nice, cool lemonade from
Mickey's refrigerator.

"What are we going to do now?" asked Daisy.

Minnie looked around. "Hmmm . . ." she said. "Maybe we could make fans. Or we could try sitting in the shade under the tree. . . ."

"Gosh! Those sprinklers look nice and cool!" said Goofy, pointing down at Mickey's lawn.

Donald nodded. "But there isn't enough water coming out of them to keep us cool!" he said.

"It's too bad the town pool doesn't open until next week," said Mickey.

As Minnie watched her friends looking at the sprinklers, she suddenly had an idea.

Minnie jumped out of her chair. "I've got it!" she shouted. "Let's go to the lake! There's always a breeze there, and there's so much to do!"

"What a great idea!" said Mickey.

"It *is* the perfect day for a swim," Daisy added.

Minnie and her friends raced home to pack. Minnie quickly threw her bathing suit, a towel, and a beach ball into her bag. Then she headed back to Mickey's house.

In no time, the friends were on their way. As they drove, they sang songs and played games. They were so excited for their day at the lake!

By the time the friends arrived, they had cooled off.

"What should we do first?" Minnie asked.

Everyone had a different idea. Daisy wanted to play basketball. Mickey and Pluto wanted to play Frisbee. And Donald wanted to go fishing!

Before anyone could stop him, Donald raced off toward a little boat docked beside the water.

Donald was already jumping into the boat when Minnie called out to him. "Wait up, Donald," she said. "I don't think we can all fit in the boat. Let's do something together!"

"But the water looks so nice!" said Donald.

"Why don't we go for a swim?" said Minnie. "We can *all* do that!"

Donald really wanted to go fishing, but finally he agreed.

After all, they *had* come to the lake to go swimming.

So the friends put away their toys and jumped into the water. . . .

"Aah," said Mickey. The water felt nice on the very hot day.

Donald leaned back and closed his eyes. "You were right, Minnie. This was a good idea!"

Minnie smiled to herself. She was glad she and her friends had found a way to cool off.

"I could stay in this water all day!" Daisy said.

And that is just what they did.

As the sun set and the day started to get cooler, Minnie and her friends got out of the water.

"I guess it's time to go home," Daisy said with a sigh.

But Minnie had one last surprise for her friends . . . s'mores!

"Gee, Minnie," said Mickey as they roasted marshmallows over a campfire, "you really do know how to plan the perfect day!"

Finally, it really was time to leave. Minnie and her friends packed their bags and got into the car.

"That was so much fun!" said Donald as they drove home. "Let's do it again tomorrow!"

# THE MISSING DAFFODILS

One spring day, Daisy Duck went to her friend Minnie's house to help in the garden. But when the two got outside, they found a big surprise.

"My daffodils!" Minnie shrieked. "They're gone! I don't understand. They were here yesterday!"

"This is terrible," Daisy said. "It must be a flower prowler!"

Minnie and Daisy searched the garden for clues.

"What's this?" Daisy asked. She pulled a few strands of fuzzy white hair off a bush near the daffodil patch.

"Maybe the flower prowler left it," Minnie said.

"Maybe," Daisy said. "Or it could be some of Figaro's hair."

A moment later, Minnie's doorbell rang. Mickey Mouse
was standing on the porch with a big bunch of daffodils! Tied
around them was a fluffy white ribbon.

"Oh, Mickey," Minnie cried. "How could you? You cut
down my daffodils!"

Mickey looked confused. "What do you mean, Minnie?" he asked. "I bought these at the flower shop because I know you love daffodils!"

"Really?" Minnie said, putting the flowers in a vase. She was glad that Mickey wasn't the flower prowler.

Minnie, Daisy, and Mickey decided to look around town for
the flower prowler. They headed to the park and found Goofy.
He was wearing a big daffodil on his vest. And he was playing with
a yo-yo that had a fuzzy white string!

"Hiya, Minnie," Goofy called. "Do you like my flower? Mr. Power is having a sale on daffodils today!"

"Hmmm . . ." said Minnie. "That's quite a coincidence."

"Maybe we'd better check out the flower shop," Daisy said.

The four friends went to Power's Flowers
and peeked through the window.

"That's Mr. Power," Mickey said.

Minnie saw that the shopkeeper had a sharp pair of scissors
and a fuzzy white mustache. And his shop was full of daffodils!

"He did it!" she cried. "I know it!"

Minnie and her friends burst into the shop. "Where did you get these daffodils?" Minnie asked.

"From a farmer named Mrs. Pote," Mr. Power answered. "She delivers daffodils here every day. But today she brought dozens of extras!"

Mr. Power pointed the way to Mrs. Pote's farm. "You can't miss her," he said. "She has fuzzy white hair."

Mrs. Pote's farm was called Pote's Goats.

"Yes, I delivered extra daffodils today," Mrs. Pote told Minnie.
"My favorite goat, Flower, usually eats a lot of them as soon as
they bloom. But she must not have been very hungry today."

That gave Minnie an idea. "May I see Flower?" she asked.

"Of course, dear," Mrs. Pote said. She led the friends to a pen. But there was no goat inside!

"Oh, my!" Mrs. Pote cried. "She must have escaped! Wherever could she have gone?"

"Look! There's a hole in the fence," Mickey said, pointing.

"Now what do we do?" Daisy exclaimed. "Not only are Minnie's daffodils gone, but so is Mrs. Pote's goat!"

"Hmmm . . ." said Minnie, deep in thought. "Maybe these two mysteries are connected!"

"What do you mean, Minnie?" Daisy asked.

"I have an idea who the flower prowler might be," Minnie explained. "It's someone who really likes daffodils. Someone who likes them even more than we do!"

Daisy held up the fuzzy strands of hair. "Don't forget this,"
she reminded Minnie. "Isn't it still a clue?"

"It sure is," Minnie agreed. "And so is this!" She pointed
toward a trail of footprints. "Follow me!"

Minnie and the others followed the footprints straight to Daisy's yard. There was Flower, happily munching away on Daisy's flowers.

"See?" Minnie said. "I knew it! There's our flower prowler. Now if we could only train her to like weeds instead!"

# MINNIE AND THE PET SHOW

"Mickey! Morty! Ferdie!" Minnie cried, racing into Mickey's backyard. "You'll never believe it! I've been chosen as chairperson for the Charity Pet Show. Isn't that exciting? We're raising money to build a new shelter for stray animals."

"A pet show?" said Morty.

"We should enter Pluto!" said Ferdie.

"Yeah! We can teach him to do tricks," said Morty. "Can we, Uncle Mickey? Please?"

"All right," Mickey said. "But only because it's for a good cause."

Mickey and Minnie watched as the boys started to train Pluto for the show.

"Roll over, Pluto," Morty said. But Pluto just wagged his tail.

"Maybe we should show him what to do," said Ferdie.

The two boys rolled over in the grass. But Pluto just stood by and watched them.

All week long, Morty and Ferdie tried to teach Pluto new tricks.

He fetched.

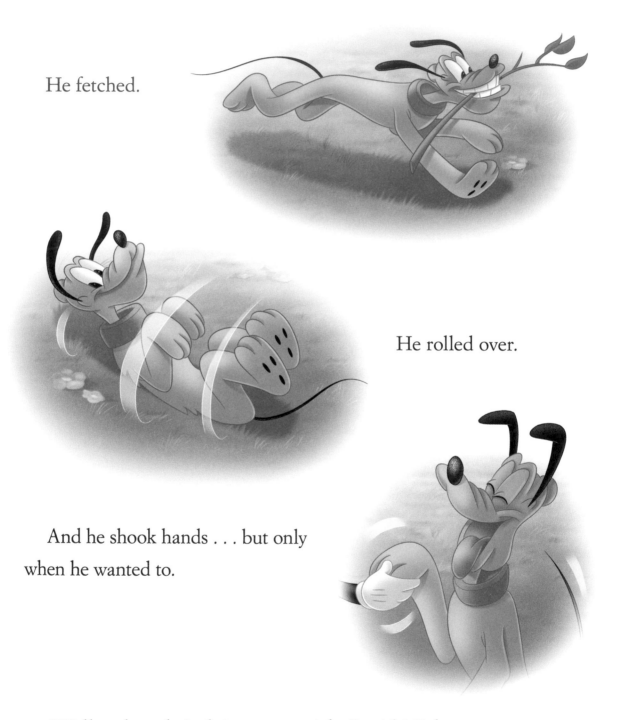

He rolled over.

And he shook hands . . . but only when he wanted to.

"Well, at least he's doing some tricks," said Mickey.

Finally, the day of the pet show arrived. Minnie was at the ticket booth when Mickey and his nephews showed up.

"Hi, Mickey," said Minnie. "Guess what! We've already made enough money for the new animal shelter!"

"That's great!" said Mickey.

What wasn't great was Pluto's performance. He shook hands when he was told to sit. He rolled over when he should have jumped. And he barked when he was supposed to lie down.

But worst of all, when Police Chief O'Hara was choosing the Best Pet of the Day, Pluto growled at him! The chief didn't know it, but he was standing right where Pluto had buried a bone!

Chief O'Hara was just about to announce the winner when
the crowd heard a scream from the ticket booth. It was Minnie!

"Help!" she cried. "Stop! Thief!"

"Oh, no! The ticket money!" Morty and Ferdie shouted.

By the time Chief O'Hara, Mickey, and the boys reached the
booth, Pluto was already sniffing around the crime scene.

"This is terrible," said Minnie. "I only walked away for a
minute! When I came back, I saw someone running away with the
cashbox."

Suddenly, Pluto stopped sniffing and ran into the woods. A moment later, Minnie heard a shout and the thief came running out of the woods. He was holding on to the cashbox—and Pluto was holding on to him!

Pluto tugged on the thief's pants. *Snap!* The thief's belt broke and he flew right into Chief O'Hara's waiting arms.

Later that afternoon, Chief O'Hara presented Pluto with the Four-Footed Hero medal.

"Thanks to Pluto, every animal will have a place to go—and a chance to find a good home," the chief said.

At home, Pluto waited by the front door for Mickey, Minnie, and the boys.

"You know," said Minnie, "it's okay that Pluto isn't a show dog. He's something better. He's a hero."

Mickey, Morty, and Ferdie agreed. And then, without being told to, Pluto shook hands with everyone because, this time, *he* wanted to.

# MINNIE'S HICCUP TRICK

**M**ickey Mouse sighed. No matter what he did, he couldn't seem to stop hiccuping.

"What's wrong, Mickey?" Minnie asked, peering over the fence.

"Oh, hiya—*hic*—Minnie," Mickey said. "It's these hiccups. They won't—*hic*—go away."

"Oh, my!" said Minnie. She thought and thought. Then she had an idea. "Daisy and I were about to go for a walk, but maybe we can help you instead."

"Help with what?" asked Daisy, walking up the garden path.

"Mickey has the hiccups!" said Minnie.

*"Hic!"* said Mickey.

Leading Mickey into the kitchen, Minnie poured him a glass of water.

"Close your eyes and take a tiny sip," she said. "Then count to five and take another sip."

Mickey closed his eyes and took a sip. Then he counted to five and took another sip.

"Did it work?" asked Daisy.

"I think it did!" said Mickey. "Thanks, Min—*hic!*"

"Hmmm . . ." said Minnie. "I think we need another idea!"

"It sounds like you need my tried-and-true hiccup cure!" said Daisy. "This may seem silly, but just do what I do."

Daisy twirled out Minnie's front door. Mickey did, too.

Daisy did two high kicks, tap-danced down the front walk, spun around once, and took a bow.

Mickey started to do the same, but halfway through—*"Hic!"*

"Maybe Donald knows a good cure for the hiccups," said Minnie. "Let's go ask him!"

The three friends set out to find Donald. But Minnie
and Daisy were much faster than Mickey. When he arrived at
Donald's house, they were waiting by the front door.

"Where's Donald?" Mickey asked.

Before Minnie could answer, Donald jumped out at Mickey.

"Boo!" he shouted.

"Aaah!" Mickey cried.

"Sorry, Mickey," Donald said. "Minnie said you have the hiccups. I thought maybe I could scare them away. Did it work?"

But Mickey just hiccuped again.

Mickey tried everything he could think of to get rid of
his hiccups. He skipped rope and sang, "M, my name is
Mickey—*hic*—I have a friend named Minnie—*hic*—and I
like mints! *Hic! Hic!*"

He stood on his head while saying the alphabet backward. *"Hic!"*

He held his nose and whistled a tune while hopping on one foot. *"Hic!"*

Nothing worked!

Mickey sat down in Donald's hammock and moped. He was starting to feel like he would never get rid of his hiccups.

"It's no use," he told his friends. "I think they're—*hic*—here to stay."

Minnie led Daisy and Donald to the side of the yard. "I have one last idea," she told them.

The three friends whispered to one another for several minutes. Finally, Donald rushed inside and returned with a large sack.

"We've got it, Mickey," Donald said. "The cure for your hiccups is right in here!"

Donald handed the sack to Minnie, who pulled out some blocks. Concentrating hard, she balanced three of them on her nose.

Next Daisy and Donald pulled two toy rings out of the sack. They hung one on each of Minnie's arms, and she began to twirl them.

"Okay, Mickey!" Minnie said. "It's your turn."

Mickey wanted to try, but all he could do was laugh.

"I'm sorry, Minnie," he said between giggles. "You just look so . . . silly!"

When Mickey finally stopped laughing, he realized
something. His hiccups were gone!

His friends waited and waited, but not another hiccup came.

"I did it!" shouted Minnie. "I cured Mickey!"

"You sure did, Minnie," said Mickey. "I guess laughter really
*is* the best medicine . . . for hiccups!"

# A SURPRISE FOR PLUTO

One sunny morning, Mickey Mouse looked out the window. "What a beautiful day!" he exclaimed. "This is perfect building weather."

His nephews, Morty and Ferdie, joined him. "What are you going to build, Uncle Mickey?" asked Morty.

Mickey's eyes twinkled. "Oh, I don't know," he said. "Maybe . . . a tree house!"

Morty and Ferdie jumped up and down. "A tree house?" Ferdie said.

"Can we help?" Morty asked.

"You would be great helpers," Mickey replied. "But there will be lots of tools in the yard. It might not be very safe. Why don't you take Pluto to the park instead?"

"Sure, Uncle Mickey!" the boys replied.

With Morty, Ferdie, and Pluto gone, Mickey called his friends. He told them all about the tree house and asked if they would like to help.

Soon Minnie, Donald, Daisy, and Goofy arrived in Mickey's yard.

"Building a tree house is a big job. Maybe we should split up the work," Mickey said. "Why don't you saw the boards, Goofy. Then Donald and I can hammer them together."

"I have an idea," Minnie said. She showed Mickey a special drawing she had made.

"Good thinking, Minnie!" Mickey replied. "That will be one of the most important jobs of all."

Goofy dumped out his toolbox in a corner of the yard.
The tools made a big *crash*—and a big mess! Goofy found what he
was looking for and began sawing the boards.

After a few minutes, Minnie walked up to him. "Sorry to
bother you, Goofy," she began. "I was wondering if you would
cut some boards for me, too?"

"Sure!" Goofy said with a grin. "Just tell me what you need."

Goofy took a look at Minnie's drawing. Then he cut some
boards and helped her carry them across the yard.

Over by the big tree, Donald and Mickey worked together to make a rope ladder. When they were finished, Mickey attached the ladder to the thickest branch. He gave the ladder a strong tug. It didn't budge.

"That should do it," Mickey said. "Once we finish building, we can use this ladder to climb into the tree house."

Just then, Goofy brought them a stack of boards. "Here you go!" he said proudly. "I still have to saw the boards for the roof, but you can use these for the floor and the walls."

"Thanks, Goofy!" Mickey said.

Mickey and Donald climbed into the tree, pulling the boards behind them. The sound of their hammers echoed through the backyard as Mickey and Donald started building.

Across the yard, Minnie pulled her hammer out of her tool belt. As she picked up the first board, she realized that she had forgotten something very important.

Minnie hurried over to the big tree. "Do you have any extra nails?" she called up. "I left all of mine at home!"

"I have some," Donald said. He fished a box of nails out of his tool belt and gave them to Minnie.

On the way back to her project, Minnie stopped to see how Daisy was doing.

"Wow, Daisy," Minnie said. "You mixed up a *lot* of paint!"

Daisy giggled. "I might have mixed a little too much," she said. "Do you need any paint for your project?"

"Thanks, Daisy," Minnie said. "That would be great!"

*Buzz-buzz-buzz* went the saw.

*Bang-bang-bang* went the hammers.

*Swish-swish-swish* went the paintbrushes.

Mickey's backyard was a very busy place!

Later that day, Morty, Ferdie, and Pluto came home from the park. Morty and Ferdie couldn't believe their eyes. "Wow!" the boys cried.

"That's the best tree house ever!" added Ferdie. Then they scrambled up the rope ladder.

But Pluto stayed behind. He tilted his head and stared at the ladder. He couldn't climb it like the others.

Mickey understood right away. "Don't worry, Pluto!" he called.
"Come around to the other side of the tree."

Pluto trotted around the tree and found something that
made his tail wag: a set of stairs that was just his size!

"Minnie made them for you," Mickey explained. "Now come
on up and join the fun!"

Pluto ran up the stairs. It really was the best tree house ever!

# SCAREDY-CAT SLEEPOVER

**M**innie Mouse rolled her pretty pink suitcase up to her best friend Daisy Duck's front door. She and Daisy were having a sleepover! The door flew open before Minnie even had a chance to ring the bell.

"Hurry up!" cried Daisy. "I've got a ton of stuff planned for us to do!"

When they got inside, Daisy announced, "First, we're making cupcakes!" The friends got right to work mixing, baking, and decorating.

"These look amazing, if I do say so myself," Daisy said.

"Tomorrow, let's leave some at Mickey's and Donald's houses as a surprise," Minnie suggested. Then she noticed the cupcakes were decorated just like the bows they were wearing. "Somehow I have a feeling they'll know the cupcakes are from us!"

Next it was time for a fashion show. Daisy brought out makeup, jewelry, and some of her most glamorous clothes.

"We are going to look so cute!" Daisy said.

When they were done, Minnie looked at herself in the mirror. "I'm not so sure about cute," she said, laughing. "I think I accidentally made myself into a Christmas tree!"

Minnie decided that "Christmas tree" was probably not the next big fashion trend. So she and Daisy ditched their new looks and changed into pajamas. It was time to relax and enjoy a movie.

"My TV gets three hundred ninety-seven channels," said Daisy. "Let's see what looks good!"

They channel surfed until they came to a scary-movie marathon.

"Perfect!" Minnie said.

A movie called *The Invisible Monster with Ten-Foot Claws* was just beginning. Minnie and Daisy watched as an actress entered a spooky mansion. The door slammed behind her with a *BANG*!

"*Eeek!*" Minnie and Daisy jumped.

"You'll never get me, monster!" the actress cried. But soon she heard the *scratch, scratch, scratch* of the monster moving toward her.

The monster chased the actress all over the house.

Luckily, she managed to escape. But Minnie and Daisy watched the rest of the movie with the lights on.

When the movie was over, the friends got ready for bed. Minnie tried not to jump every time she heard a strange sound. Daisy tried to ignore the creepy shadows on the wall. Soon they climbed into bed and wished each other sweet dreams.

But an hour later, they were still awake.

"That movie scared me," Minnie finally admitted. "Somehow an invisible monster is even worse than one you can see. Just imagining what it might look like gave me goose bumps!"

"I got goose bumps, too," replied Daisy. She tried to cheer up her friend by making a joke. "Especially when that girl wore the ugly sweater with mustard-yellow sparkles. I've never seen anything so frightening!"

Minnie suggested they drink some warm milk to make themselves sleepy. After two big mugs full, they were back in bed . . . and still awake.

"It's not working," Daisy groaned. "What should we do now?"

"How about counting sheep?" Minnie replied. She closed her eyes and began picturing a meadow full of them.

Daisy closed her eyes, too, but she decided to count other things instead.

Finally, the girls started to drift off. Then, suddenly, they heard a loud *SCRATCH*!

"What was that?" Daisy cried.

"I don't know," Minnie said, huddling under her blanket. "Maybe it was just a branch scraping against the window?"

"Yes, that must be it," replied Daisy, but she wasn't convinced.

A few minutes later, they heard more scratching, and then
a loud *SCREECH*!

"*Aaaahhh!*" yelled the girls.

"What if it's the Invisible Monster with Ten-Foot Claws?"
asked Daisy.

Minnie took a deep breath. "Let's try to stay calm," she
said. "I'm sure whatever is making those noises is perfectly
harmless—and there's only one way to find out."

"What's that?" asked Daisy.

"We have to be like the girl in the movie and investigate," said Minnie.

"Okay." Daisy nodded nervously. "But I'm not dressing like her!"

So the pair tiptoed toward the sound of the scratching.
It seemed to be coming from outside the front door.

"Let's peek out the window," suggested Daisy. "Maybe we
can see something."

Minnie pulled aside the curtain and let out a loud gasp.

"What is it?" asked Daisy.

"Kittens!" cried Minnie.

She quickly threw open the door and brought them inside.

"Poor things. Do you think they're lost?" Daisy asked.

"Maybe," Minnie replied. "We'll ask around the
neighborhood tomorrow and see if they belong to anyone."

"In the meantime, I'll make up the spare bed," said Daisy.

"What spare bed?" Minnie wondered.

Daisy grabbed her laundry basket. "This one!" she said.

"Who would have guessed that our monster would turn out to be furry and cute?" Minnie asked as she snuggled back into her bed.

"Not me!" Daisy replied, and the two girls burst into giggles.

Just a few minutes later, Minnie, Daisy, and the not-so-scary kittens were all fast asleep!

# A NICE DAY FOR A SAIL

Mickey and Minnie were relaxing in the park when Huey, Dewey, and Louie appeared in their sailboat. "Hiya, Mickey. Hiya, Minnie," the boys said. "Nice day for sailing, isn't it?" Mickey and Minnie nodded and waved to the boys as they sailed away.

Suddenly, Mickey had an idea. "Say, Minnie," he said. "It *is* a nice day for sailing." Mickey pointed to a boat tied up by the water. "How about we go for a ride, too?"

"I would love to," Minnie said with a smile. "A nice, easy ride sounds like the perfect way to spend the day."

Mickey and Minnie climbed into the boat and began to row away from shore. They had not gone far when a squirrel leaped into the boat with them! Startled, Mickey and Minnie jumped back . . . and landed right in the water.

Mickey and Minnie climbed back into the boat and rowed
to shore.

"How about a little lunch while we dry off?" Mickey
suggested.

Minnie thought that was a wonderful idea. Soon the two
were relaxing in the sun with hot dogs.

As they were enjoying their lunch, Pluto came running by. Seeing the hot dogs, he decided he wanted one, too. He jumped into Mickey's lap and tried to grab the food.

"Stop it, boy!" cried Mickey.

"Pluto," said Minnie. "If you want a hot dog, we can get you one of your own."

But it was too late. Pluto knocked Mickey and Minnie right into the water.

Donald Duck was nearby in his speedboat and saw what
happened. He helped Mickey and Minnie into his boat. "Why
don't you ride with me for a while?" he said. "You can take it
easy and let the engine do the work."

Mickey and Minnie sat back and relaxed, listening to the happy *putt-putt* of the engine. They had just reached the middle of the lake when the boat's engine suddenly stopped.

"What do we do now?" Minnie asked.

"I have an idea," Donald said. He took off his hat and started to paddle with it.

Mickey and Minnie did the same. Huffing and puffing, they made their way back to shore.

Back on shore, Huey, Dewey, and Louie had finished their sail. "Do you want to borrow our boat?" Huey asked Minnie. "There's a nice wind today."

Minnie thought. "I guess we could *try* sailing one more time," she said.

And so Mickey and Minnie set off in the boys' boat. But after a few minutes, the wind stopped blowing.

"Oh, no!" Mickey groaned. "We're stranded again!"

Mickey and Minnie tried to paddle with their hands, but it was no use. They just kept going in circles. "What are we going to do now?" asked Minnie.

Suddenly, Mickey looked up. Goofy and Donald were coming
toward them in rowboats.

"We thought you might need some help," said Donald.

"Hyuck," said Goofy. "How about a tow to shore?"

As the sun began to set over the peaceful lake, Mickey
and Minnie sat back and smiled. They had finally gotten their
nice, easy boat ride!

# THE BRAVEST DOG

It was a sunny day. Minnie Mouse was sunbathing in her backyard when she saw Mickey run out of his house and toward his car.

"Mickey, where are you going?" Minnie asked.

"Oh, Minnie, it's terrible," Mickey said. "A circus train was going through town and some of the animals got lost! The sheriff asked me to help find them before they cause trouble."

Mickey quickly climbed into his car. Pluto tried to follow, but Mickey stopped him. "You stay here with Minnie," he said, and drove away.

Mickey had not been gone long when Pluto began to tug at Minnie's skirt.

Minnie smiled. She knew exactly what Pluto wanted to do.

"Oh, all right, Pluto," she said. "It's not very likely that we'll run into any of the animals, and it is a nice day for a walk."

So Minnie followed Pluto down the path to the river.

Minnie and Pluto had not gone far when they heard a
hissing sound coming from behind a log.

"Eek!" Minnie cried. "Snakes! They must have escaped
from the circus train!"

But Pluto was not afraid of snakes. With a snarl, he
pounced into the grass . . . and found a small orange cat and
her six kittens.

"Oops," Minnie said with a giggle. "I guess it wasn't snakes
after all. Come on, Pluto, let's not disturb her."

Minnie stayed close to Pluto after that. If there were any loose snakes, she didn't want to run into them.

"It would be fun to find a bear cub, though," said Minnie. "Or a seal. I love seals! I wonder if one could come this far."

Suddenly, Minnie and Pluto heard a splashing sound coming from the river. Before Minnie could stop him, Pluto dashed down a hill and plunged into the cold water.

Minnie was right behind him. "Be careful, Pluto!" she cried.

But it was not a seal splashing around in the water. It was
a little puppy who had fallen in!

Pluto laid the puppy at Minnie's feet.

"A cat and a puppy!" Minnie laughed, scratching Pluto
behind the ears. "We'd better not tell anyone about our
wild-animal hunting!"

"It's okay, Pluto," Minnie said as the two walked back to Mickey's house. "I love you even if you never capture anything wilder than a wet puppy."

Minnie turned to Pluto. "You know," she said, "what you need is a big bone! Why don't we go find one for you?"

But when Minnie and Pluto walked into Mickey's kitchen, they found that it was a disaster. Milk had been spilled all over the table, broken dishes littered the floor, and one of the windows was open!

"Oh, Pluto!" Minnie cried. "Someone has been in here! What if it was one of the circus animals? It could still be here. What should we do?"

Snarling, Pluto sniffed around the kitchen for a trail. Finally, with a loud bark, he leaped through the open window and raced across the yard to the woodshed.

"Be careful, Pluto," Minnie called. "Whatever it is may be dangerous!"

Just then, Mickey pulled up.

"Oh, Mickey," Minnie said, "something broke into your kitchen! Pluto is tracking it!"

Minnie pointed to the shed, where Pluto was slowly nosing through the door. As he disappeared inside, Minnie held her breath. What would Pluto find?

Long moments passed. Then, slowly, the shed door
opened again and Pluto came out. But he was not alone.
On his back was a tiny monkey dressed in a little hat and vest.

"Pluto, you did it!" Mickey said. "You found the last
missing circus animal!"

Mickey laughed as the monkey jumped into his arms. "Maybe this little guy isn't so wild after all," he said. "But it took a lot of courage to go into the woodshed after him."

"Pluto has been brave all day," Minnie told Mickey.

A few minutes later, Pluto was sitting beside the circus's ringmaster. He and Mickey had returned the monkey to him. "Thanks, Pluto," the ringmaster said. "The show couldn't have gone on without you!"

# MINNIE AND THE DUDE RANCH

**M**innie Mouse was excited. She, Mickey, and Goofy were going to the Lucky Star Dude Ranch. But Mickey was still packing.

"Come on, Mickey!" Minnie shouted to Mickey. "I want to learn how to ride a horse!"

"Be right there, Minnie," Mickey shouted downstairs as he put the last of his clothing in his suitcase.

Goofy was excited to ride a horse, too. The minute they reached the ranch, he hopped on the first horse he saw. But he jumped on it backward!

"Uh-oh!" Goofy cried as the horse bucked. "Now what do I do?"

Luckily, Minnie had brought a bunch of carrots with her to feed the horses. She held one out to the horse and he happily trotted over to eat it.

"Whew! That was close!" Goofy gasped. "Thank goodness you were here, Minnie!"

Minnie and her friends went inside to change into their riding clothes. When they came back out, the owner of the ranch was waiting for them. "Howdy, cowgirl," he said to Minnie. "I'm Cowboy Bob. How 'bout we get you up on that horse?"

Cowboy Bob helped Minnie onto a horse. In no time she was riding like a pro.

"This isn't so hard," said Goofy a little while later as he trotted by on a horse. "Hey, Cowboy Bob, can you teach me how to use a lasso?"

"You betcha, Goofy," Cowboy Bob said. "Just swing the rope over your head, like this. Then aim and let go!"

Goofy hopped off his horse and tried to follow Cowboy Bob's example. "I'm going to lasso that hitching post," he said.

Goofy whirled the lasso and let go. But instead of catching the post, he caught his foot!

"Whoops!" Goofy cried.

"Looks like you could use some more practice, Goofy,"
Mickey said.

Minnie giggled. "Mickey and I are going to go for a ride,"
she said. "We'll see you when you get yourself untangled, Goofy."

For three days, Minnie, Mickey, and Goofy learned how to be cowboys. On their last morning at the ranch, they planned to watch the rodeo.

Cowboys from all over gathered to watch the show. Minnie and Goofy sat in the stands. "I wonder where Mickey is," said Minnie, watching. "He really wanted to see this!"

But Mickey was still asleep! He had forgotten to set his alarm clock.

As the noisy crowd passed by his window, it woke him up. Mickey looked at the time. He had to hurry or he would miss all the fun!

Mickey quickly got dressed and dashed out the door. He raced across a field, jumped over a fence . . . and landed right on a bucking bronco in the middle of the rodeo!

Everyone cheered as Mickey held tightly to the reins.

"Hey! This is sort of fun!" he cried.

As Mickey waved his hat to the crowd, the announcer cried out, "Mickey Mouse has just broken the ranch record for the longest-ever bronco ride!"

Just then, the bronco bucked again and Mickey slid off him.

"Oh, no!" Minnie shouted. "We have to help Mickey!"

"I'll lasso it for you, Mickey!" shouted Goofy. But instead of
lassoing the bronco, he lassoed Mickey.

Meanwhile, Minnie hopped over the fence and led the bronco
safely back to his stall.

Later that day, the crowd cheered as Cowboy Bob presented the rodeo ribbons.

Minnie won for taking good care of the horses. Mickey won for his bronco riding. And Goofy won for trying to lasso everything in sight!

Later that night, Minnie sat by the campfire with her friends.

"This has been so much fun," she said. "I can't believe we have to leave tomorrow!"

Just then, Minnie spotted an odd shape against the moon. "Hey, look! A coyote! Now I really feel like a cowgirl!"

"Want me to lasso him?" asked Goofy.

Minnie giggled. "Thanks, Goofy, but I think he's better off where he is!"

And with another giggle, she went back to enjoying the campfire.

# A PERFECT PICNIC

It was a beautiful spring day. The sun was shining. The birds were singing. And Mickey Mouse was planning a picnic.

Suddenly, Mickey had an idea. "I should invite our friends to join us," he told Pluto.

Mickey picked up the phone and called Minnie. "Hiya, Minnie," he said. "How would you like to join me and Pluto for a picnic in the park? We can all share lunch."

Minnie agreed to join Mickey and went to pack her picnic
basket. Meanwhile, Mickey called the rest of his friends and
invited them to come, too.

"Oh, Pluto," Mickey said as he packed Pluto's Frisbee. "This
will be so much fun! We can all enjoy the sunshine together and
share our favorite foods!"

Mickey was about to leave his house when Pluto began barking at him. Pluto grabbed Mickey's shorts and began to tug on them.

Mickey followed Pluto into the kitchen. "Thanks for reminding me," he said, taking out a bone. "I wouldn't want to forget your lunch!"

Over at Minnie's house, things were not going so well.
Minnie had packed all of her favorite foods: a peanut butter
sandwich, lemonade, and an apple. But as she got ready to
leave, she started to wonder if she would like the lunches her
friends had packed.

I don't want to share my lunch, she thought. I want to eat
it myself!

Donald, Daisy, and Goofy felt the same way. They had all packed their favorite foods. But what if they didn't like what their friends had packed? Maybe it was better not to share lunches after all.

Mickey didn't know that his friends had changed their minds. Excited about their picnic, he filled his wagon and began to walk toward the park.

When he got there, he found his friends waiting for him. They all had baskets of food. But they didn't look very happy.

"What's wrong?" Mickey asked his friends.

"I don't want to share my lunch," Donald said.

"What if I don't like the lunch I get?" asked Minnie.

Daisy and Goofy agreed. Everyone wanted to eat their own favorite foods.

"Oh," Mickey said, disappointed. "I guess we don't *have* to share."

Minnie looked at Mickey. He looked so sad. She didn't want to be the reason he was upset!

Minnie handed Mickey her picnic basket. "It's okay, Mickey," she said. "I'll trade lunches with you. I'm sure I'll like whatever you packed."

"Really? Thanks, Minnie!" Mickey said.

Mickey's friends saw how happy Minnie had made Mickey.
They wanted to make Mickey happy, too.

"Will someone trade lunches with me?" Donald asked,
holding out his basket.

Daisy took Donald's lunch. Then she handed her basket to
Goofy and he gave his basket to Donald.

Mickey laid out a blanket, and the friends got to work setting up their picnic.

Minnie passed out plates.

Goofy handed out napkins.

Daisy gave everyone a cup.

And Donald set out forks.

Finally, it was time to eat!

Mickey opened his picnic basket first. When he saw what was inside, he started to laugh.

"What's so funny, Mickey?" Minnie asked. Then she looked in her basket and started to laugh, too.

Everyone had packed peanut butter sandwiches and lemonade!

The only difference in the baskets was the fruit.

Daisy had grapes.

Minnie had an orange.

Goofy had a banana.

Mickey had an apple.

And Donald had a pineapple!

"Isn't there some way we can share our fruit?" asked Minnie.

"I have an idea," said Mickey. "Leave it to me."

While his friends ate their sandwiches and drank their lemonade, Mickey cut up the fruit. He put it all in a bowl and mixed it together. Then he brought the bowl back over to the blanket. He had made a big fruit salad!

"What a great idea," Minnie said as Mickey passed out the fruit salad.

"Now we can all try each other's favorite fruits!" Daisy added.

Donald nodded. "Thanks for inviting us, Mickey," he said.

As Mickey's friends settled down to enjoy
the rest of their picnic, they realized that Mickey
had been right. Sharing *was* fun, after all!

# MINNIE'S MISSING RECIPE

Mickey Mouse was relaxing in his living room when the doorbell rang. Mickey opened the door. Outside was a very panicked Minnie.

"Gee, what's wrong, Minnie?" Mickey asked.

"Oh, Mickey, it's awful," said Minnie. "Today is the annual Bake-Off and I can't find my cinnamon swirl cake recipe!"

Just then, Pluto ran up the driveway. He dropped a rolled-up paper at Mickey's feet and began to bark.

"Thanks, Pluto," Mickey said. "But right now we have to help Minnie. Come on!"

Back at Minnie's house, Mickey searched the kitchen. But the recipe was nowhere to be found.

"It was on the counter this morning," Minnie said. "I don't know what could have happened!"

Suddenly, Mickey noticed a postcard on the floor. "What's this?" he asked.

Minnie giggled. "Donald came over this morning to show me his postcard collection. He was so excited to show me his newest ones that he dropped the whole stack on the counter. That one must have fallen on the floor."

That gave Mickey an idea. "Maybe Donald accidentally picked up your recipe with his other postcards. Let's go ask him!"

Mickey, Minnie, and Pluto headed over to Donald's house.
But when they got there, they found Donald angrily pacing his
living room.

"What's wrong, Donald?" Minnie asked.

"It's my new postcards! They're missing!"

Donald showed Mickey and Minnie his postcard collection. "See? Five of them are missing!"

"I'm missing my cinnamon swirl cake recipe, too!" said Minnie.

"We were wondering if you might have picked it up by accident when you were at Minnie's this morning," Mickey said.

As Donald stared sadly at his postcard collection, Pluto dropped the rolled-up paper on the table. But Donald was too upset to notice.

"Where was the last place you saw your postcards?" Mickey asked.

Donald thought. "I was flipping through them when I came back from Minnie's house," he said. "I came through the door . . . and tripped over Huey! The boys were working on a collage in the hallway!"

"Oh, my!" said Minnie. "You don't think they accidentally used some postcards in their collage, do you?"

Pluto barked and dropped the paper at Minnie's feet.

"Thanks, Pluto," said Minnie. "But we have to solve this mystery!"

And with that, Minnie, Mickey, Donald, and Pluto went to wait for the boys at the bus stop.

"Boys," Donald said when his nephews got off the school bus. "Did you use my postcards in your collage?"

Donald's nephews blushed. "Those were yours, Uncle Donald?" Huey asked.

"We thought they were pieces of junk mail," Dewey said.

"Junk mail!" cried Donald angrily.

"Now, now," said Minnie calmly. "It was just an accident, Donald." Then she turned to Huey, Dewey, and Louie. "Where is the collage now?" she asked the boys.

Louie shrugged. "It's the strangest thing," he said. "I rolled it up and put it in my backpack this morning."

"But when we got on the bus, it was gone," Dewey said.

"It must have fallen out somewhere between Donald's house and the bus stop," Minnie said.

The group searched everywhere, from the bus stop all the way back to Donald's house. They even checked Mickey's and Minnie's yards. But they couldn't find the collage anywhere.

Pluto whined and dropped his rolled-up paper at Huey's feet.

"Hey!" Huey shouted, looking down. "This is it! Pluto had it all along!"

"We must have dropped it in Mickey's yard after all," said Dewey.

"And Pluto found it!" said Louie.

The boys unrolled the paper and showed off their collage—complete with Donald's postcards and Minnie's missing recipe!

Minnie giggled. "You were trying to help us all along, Pluto!" she said. "I'm going straight home to bake two cinnamon swirl cakes. One for the contest and one for you!"

And that is just what she did!